Hell's Press Presents

First paperback edition 2023

ISBN   978-1-7381321-2-6 (paperback)
ISBN   978-1-7381322-1-8   (ebook)

Fairie Tales

Rumpelstiltzkin , Goldilocks

COUNT FATHOM

Dedicated to...

...you, getting yourself out from that miserable condition of war which is necessarily consequent to the natural passions of men when there is no visible power to keep them in awe, and tie them by fear of punishment to the performance of their covenants.

A contract you want, and you have it, you slave. I cannot abide it, I'll live in a cave. Nature red in tooth and claw, Nuck will take you in her paw, for men are evil with their law, submit we do in fear and awe. To the cave I will withdraw.

Listen more, do I, when I am told that wolves are lurking in the fold, deceivers in the darkness, cloaked in secrecy. Endeavour, do they, by dark and erroneous doctrines, to extingguish in them the light, by confederacy. One is wrong and one is right by turns of fate's foul mystery.

Inspired by Thomas Hobbes

TABLE OF CONTENTS

Preface

Shut the door! Don't let them in. They're crowding all around. Crouch down low and hold your breath, beware the slightest sound. Lurking in the bushes and hiding in the trees, eyes are hiding everywhere, these busy little bees. Watch the dance these bees do make, the furor they are in. It's crap, it's trash, it's second rate, It's sacrilege, it's sin. Follow, then, if what you like is what has come before. I feel something deep inside is asking of me more. For those upset, I understand. Please politely use the door.

Open wide the rabbit hole for those that stay inside. A grip upon the edge I have, my foot lodged firm across, arch my back with effort, knuckles dug deep in the moss. Strain I will with all I can, all force must be applied.

In you go, and I behind, down to a realm of mind. What is it that will be inside, what is it that we'll find? More things there are in hell and Earth than dreamt of by our kind. A patient hand is needed for this tangle to unwind.

Rumpelstiltzkin

Hark! Ye that have ears to hear, of a time before things had names. Came one of our kind upon the manifestation of evil. Horrorstricken, petrified, he raised a rebelling arm, pointed determinedly at the incarnate evil and yawped "Nuck!"

Evil winced painfully at the name. Fear though he did, our man felt strength. Named then she needn't be so feared. Isolated from all others, Nuck had nowhere to hide. She could not escape the light. She could be seen and called, and her powers were greatly diminished thereby.

Nuck was furious. The man must suffer. She had him bound to a post in a clearing in a valley within the vale. There he remained, fixed to his post, where he suffered the darkest despair. The man strained to maintain his mental balance. But time is merciless, and he would lapse into episodes of psychotic violence, shaking and rattling his post in his agony. Thus evil came to know the man.

Nuck's face contorted into her wicked smile, she raised a bony finger and proclaimed "Rumpelstiltzkin!" and his name was written in the book of the damned by evil herself. All hope was lost. Slowly, but inevitably, he was stripped bare of all vestiges of goodness and virtue. He felt a cold greed take possession of his soul. Nuck had infected him with an insatiable thirst for wealth. Avarice was evil's most terrible curse.

Rumpelstiltzkin would wander the earth, poisoned with a rapacious appetite, taking what he could even from those least able to afford the loss, spreading misery and woe throughout our kind. This is the price he pays for knowing evil.

Not so very long ago our world was ruled by Kings. Some may argue it still is. Much pleasure to you. We won't be indulging you this evening. The land of the King would be parcelled out to nobles in stewardship. In return our nobles would collect tax from their people to satisfy the requirements of the crown, among other obligations such as soldiery and safe passage for trade through his lands. But before even this time of Kings, was yet another. Dear modern reader, are you prepared?

The strong were both feared and admired, for they were strong. The village relied for protection upon the strength of the few. One village was indeed very strong for the strength of one man alone. Wigana, was his name. Loud Wigana he was called. He compelled obedience from his neighbours, and with the tribute paid him, afforded an army of some considerable number.

Tribute is taxation. Tribute is theft. Both are true. Security and administration under compulsion is an end to freedom. She did not die with a whisper. Wigana ruled with strength, murdering those who oppose, and collecting his due. Loud Wigana.

One man is the tip of a spear. But he must relegate authority to administer his law. This he did, entrusting the custody of rule over a generous, though bandit plagued and corrupt eastern province, rife with dissent and disorder, to an ally. Freedom would die at the hands of Ikarl for these troublesome independent lands.

In turn Ikarl pillaged the peoples of the east, suffocating them down to the merest subsistence, at the mercy of his tyranny. While Wigana waited patiently, Ikarl refused to offer even partial plunder, claiming the expense of his ever growing force required his entire purse. Ikarl profited handsomely, and was proclaimed locally as King of the East.

The King in his cart sits mountains apart from the masses he tramples beneath. His courtiers and guards, his ministers and bards, graciously baring their teeth. What the King may desire, his soldiers acquire, so the King may most generously unsheathe. Once he is done what he has just begun, the King feels a glorious relief.

A lawless land requires a vigilant and threatening oversight. Thus Ikarl would personally oversee much trade within his purview. Our ruthless tyrant prototype was at this very moment considering the prospects of a Miller, sat squat at the intersection of several villages in the land. All grain for many leagues around brought their stores to be milled by this man. Yet he lived in but a modest comfort. Avarice and ambition are sternly suspicious of innocence and permissiveness.

Walked he, Ikarl, this day to the step before the miller's shop, yet stopped short at the sight in the slanting of light of a pulse of a bright brilliant beauty. This golden shine, he thought, must be mine. With a lustful grin veiled thin to begin let us enter the plot of our tale.

"Good King Ikarl! As a child I played along the riverside with your mother's sister's husband's cousin, Dieter. And here we are together! Of all the hundreds of people I've ever seen in my life, here you are! Who would believe it?"

"Miller, you've done well for yourself I see."

"On this grain business I lose money most of the time. The small farmers, you see, they can't afford my share or they will starve through the winter. I forgo their fees so often that most of the time the mill is turning at a loss. But I have a secret that helps me muddle by. My daughter, a very special girl you see, can spin straw into gold. And so we get by. Hehehe.." Our affable miller was clearly nervous, but chanced familiarity to rescue him from Nuck's malevolence to strangers.

"Miller, I am a direct man. Where is my share of the proceeds of your trade? I will take them now and go, leaving my grace and protection to your family."

"As I told you, dear, King, I have only enough to eat for myself and my daughter. Please!"

"Call your daughter, miller."

The sweating miller cracked falsetto as he dared not pause, and called to his daughter, "Ludmila!"

Slowly out from a creaking door on the second floor stept our sweet young victim, innocence, grace and charm to the slaughter. Down the stair came she swift and fair, with the freedom of air, to be so suddenly ensnared by a captor. Ikarl seized the stunned belle by her wrist and, though she did resist, he would persist, and mounted her behind him on his horse. The miller was hoarse, dazed and displaced, upset and confused, left badly abused by Ikarl the King of the land.

Pricked off at a terrific pace, the pair proceeded upon the path to the Palace. The miller's daughter was not an unwelcome burden, far from it. Ikarl enjoyed immensely the rhythmic prance of his filly, sometimes slowing her down to an oh so gentle, maddeningly measured hip sway, then prick the spurs into a dancing trot, the girl pressed close for comfort and profit. All pretty things know men.

Into the Palace courtyard they rode and Ludmila was dragged once again, for Ikarl was appreciative but not forgiving, up and around the spiral stair tower to a room with a store of straw. Mound upon mound spread thick on the ground, Ludmila looks down to evade the King's frown. "Spin gold from that bed, and I'll give you some bread." the King said, and in they did bring a stool and a sound spinning wheel.

The door shut once and firmly. Ludmila collapsed into the hay, resigned to her helpless fate. Is there no one that cares about Ludmila? Her senseless capture at the hands of a budding tyrant? This impossible injustice? The miller cares. But he can do nothing. The strong will enforce their law. Nuck cares. Nuck took pleasure in the shadows of misfortune she casts across life.

A pulse shivers the shadows suddenly, beyond a corner in the room. Manifest before her becomes the queerest creature ever seen. He was shrivelled and hunched, gaunt and pale, sly and anxious, mischievous but merry, merry but unstably so. His hood pulled back revealing wisps of tonsure, a spare hair tiara about this fallen Prince that dared to name Nuck. High sharp cheekbones sat beside his sunken blacken eyes, decorated beneath by a protruding hook nose, bending to touch its mirrored counterpart, the chin. All was moulded into a deathly complexion of clay, all clothed in a husk of sack and rope.

11

"Look at the sad girl make water! A man's mouth may lose him a daughter. Your fortunes are dire, my dear. I have a proposition for you to hear. Would you like to live long, a life filled with song, and riches and health and never cause to fear?"

"Oh, yes, sir! Whatever will I do? This straw must be spun into gold or the King pulls off my pretty head. I'm at your mercy, sir!"

"Then I am your saviour. I will this very night spin the straw to gold. In return you will part with that alluring necklace you hold."

"My mother's pearls? She's dead you know. That's Nuck."

"The pearls or you die!" an enraged eruption from a hopping red elf man heated the room.

Ludmila fingered the pearls of her ancestral heirloom. "I agree."

The little man clapped his hands and cackled with brilliant delight. He hopped onto the stool before the spinning wheel and began to feed it the straw hand over hand while pumping vigorously at the pedal, and out the other side strands of gold began to pile at their feet. Faster and faster worked the goblin man while the gold thread gathered. He continued to work feverishly until the moon reached its zenith, and the last of the straw had been spun.

Wiping the sweat from his brow, the imp hopped off the stool, strafed back and forth in front of the sleeping Ludmila, finally snatching at the pearl necklace, tearing it from her neck, and vanishing into the darkness of his corner.

Ludmila awoke in awe of the heaps of gold thread, but inconsolable for the grief of her loss. The King came. Unable to restrain the acquisitive impulse, he had some guards place our poor Ludmila into an even larger larder loaded yet more heavily with stores of straw. He called through the closing door, "Spin this straw and I will most certainly spare your life and that of your thieving father, my dear."

Within a moment of finding herself alone once again, Ludmila skipped, in a game of corners, about the room calling out.

"Elf man! Elf man! Where are you hiding? Great goblin relieve me of suffering and woe! I have but one treasure to offer

your honour, my most cherished token,
may it be worthy of your favours. This ring
on my finger was a gift from Wigana, who
swore it once graced a bishop in Rome.
Please take this in trade for the spinning
of wonders and free this poor bird to go
home!"

The shadows shivered opposite our
girl, forming into our avaricious imp, hopping bow legged, foot to foot with wonder-
ful speed and agility, cackling merrily all the
while.

"I'll spin the whole lot for that bishop's rot and free this sparrow from harm. Lie
down now, tot, and let not in your thoughts
of troubles and worries alarm. Your saviour
I'll be once again, and then in the end we'll
settle our fee."

An glowing yellow dawn spread lustre about the golden room as Ludmila awoke to wonder yet surpassed. Towers of gold thread bound about in every corner. The bishop's ring has vanished, and the door to her turret cell opens to reveal King Ikarl of the East. Elated at the immensity of fortune's favours, he once more locks our Princess in yet another warehouse, stacked with straw for the stables, here for winter storage.

"My dear, my darling, my love, my queen! What a strange and tangled torture our love has been. Such wonders as yours the world has never yet seen. Once more, my dear, my darling, we'll marry next day! Once more, I beg you, to an empire your love paves the way!"

Alone before the impossible once again, Ludmila had nought to do but call for fortune's favour, in a growing fever of anxious torment. Appeared from the fog of the darkness and shadow evil's most awful disease, an appetite voracious, unsleeping, unfettered, infecting the world at Nuck's ease.

"I've nothing to offer! Oh what shall I do? My great goblin saviour, please have pity and ask of me what I can afford. I am desperate and at your mercy, my lord!"

Bent, now, to hands and knees is the tortured wicked soul of man, so hollowed with greed that it serves as his only satisfaction. The face of evil sits still, staring intently into the eyes of our poor impoverished princess, as he decides what to take.

"I will spin this straw to gold in one single night, while you sleep, dear girl. You will be saved, you will marry this King and you will become Queen. In time you will bear him a child. This child you owe to me. I will return soon after the birth to conclude our agreement. You are saved, princess, and you will live long and in comfort. Now sleep."

Under threat of death what will man not sacrifice? Must we stand stalwart, shoulder to shoulder with our principles and virtues at death's most pressing advance? And if we are permitted moral flexibility in times of mortal crises, then how far will this benevolent laxity allow us to slide? If the risk is great to one's survival, some amount of self interest at perhaps minor cost to others can be argued legitimate. An worthy discussion, an web of irreducible complexity, an conundrum. Go and seek an answer so you can begin to be what you now consider yourself.

Ludmila slept soundly and well, waking to a hark and a knock on the door. The king, in three steps, came to his knees, hands clasped, preserving what dignity and composure he could as he fell weeping in joy to the cold stone floor of the storeroom. Ludmila became wife to King Ikarl and Queen in the East that very day.

Won't the animals go hungry now that their feed has become gold? Good Queen Luddy saw to the purchase of grain and straw and sundry other goods from all the land. Merchants, farmers, artisans, and tradesmen of all sorts wore heavy pockets on their pants. Having only converted a modest fraction of their gold to coin and sending it out amongst the towns and villages of the province, Ludmila had invigorated the land. Queen Luddy embraced change. She sought engineering solutions to all the questions her people might face. Fertilization and land management increased yields. Water flows were successfully diverted, permanent reservoirs created, and fish catch counted and measured. Jurisprudence was forced to wield a pen that would restrain the sword. Ikarl's security force established an more formal working bureaucracy with restrictions and safeguards to protect the people, and regular patrol of public ways to ensure safe passage for goods and persons throughout the land. Despite the burden of taxation, the people and their rulers prospered.

An abundance was created. In the autumn harvest of her third year as Queen of the East, Ludmila bore child. Throughout her term she oscillated between anxious and frantic, worrying the palace physician into peevish prognostications. Days passed after the birth and the Queen's dementia improved, but was replaced by an suffocating depression. Moons swung on a rope round about the earth, as the earth did about the sun, and the child loved by misery grew bathed in tears.

In late summer of the child's first year, a fierce heat flooded the land from the west, burning the crops before harvest had begun. From murders of scavenging blackbirds, to swarms of locusts that blot out the sun, and a rain of frogs falling splat from the sky after a thunderous storm, ill omen beset King Ikarl into autumn.

Night fell early on the tenth day of the tenth month as a blanket of black cloud covered the earth in shadow. Candles walked wearily through the dark silence of the sweating palace walls. One such light was lifted by the hand of the Queen herself, shook from her sleep by a clap of thunder, and stirred by faint whispers from the thick of the dark. Always and ever but steps just ahead of her, Luddy was lured with a snap. Through rooms and through halls, she heeds evil's call to spring her malevolent trap.

Opening now the heavy door of the storeroom, the vanishing light of her candle blew through the stores of hay and illuminated the elf man, head bowed, seated on a stool before the miller's daughter once again.

"I have come for the child."

"You mustn't!" The Queen pleaded.

A sudden rage erupted from the dwarf, as his face boiled, he leapt clear his height and plunged violently into the stones, cracking one considerably with the stomp of his tiny foot.

"The child is mine, you slithering slime! I'll curse your whole family disease! Famine and drought, hobbled with gout, you'll scrape and you'll beg on your knees! You're nothing! You're crap! You're wretched and foul! And I will enslave your miserable soul!"

"Great Goblin grant me one last gasp of hope before you drown me in the ocean of despair! I beg of you, for anything that I have to give, it is yours! I have riches beyond counting. Gems the size of a child's foot. Ancient and powerful amulets, rings and bracelets. I can satisfy your heed, your greed, your every need, but let my child alone!"

"My patience stretches thin! Your treasures now are worthless tin. The child I'll take and make it mine, ere love will conquer Nuck in time. I'll cast aside the chains and purse, and lift from under evil's curse. We made a bargain, you and I, And you will honour thy word!"

"I will not break my oath. Find favour in your cruelty, and do with me what you will, but grant me this last flicker of time!"

"In the dark of night, when the raven takes flight from your window sill, Princess, you'll come. With child in your arms, no tricks or cheap charms, you will hand the child over to me. Defy me once more and me dear I assure you my mercy will not match my wrath."

The elf evaporated into the shadowed walls, the echo of his evil heartbeat started a stuttered reverberation rippling through the castle stones. That night Ludmila, Queen of the East, clutched close to her child, weeping the child to worry. Morning came and the Queen would not part from the girl. Worry progressed to hysteria, and the child suffered. The Queen allowed the child to be taken from her and, in a tense fever, the Queen went on a walk through the tangled paths of the woods as the sun receded beyond the rolling hills.

The night forest suffocates the Queen in darkness, yet her steps are quick, with a nervous anxiety. Would she know were the wither and where of her wanderings whispered to her from whence the fates weave their wonders? Through the growth guarding a path the Queen pushes, passing into a glade by a stream. A hill by the stream has been seen in a dream. An homely hovel has been shovelled quite snugly just there. From the far side of the home spies the Queen a small fire. And then the small elf man unplugging a jug!

A stumble, a hop, a skip and a shake, the goblin stomps madly, the ground beneath quakes. "Tonight, tonight my plans I make. Tomorrow, tomorrow the baby I take. The Queen, she blunders away this game, for she knows not the power to claim by the forcing out of evil's name!"

The goblin hopped about the fire, stewed in jug liquor, crouching and rubbing his palms together, then erupting into wild eyed fervor, and shooting another swig of his goblin juice to compliment his dance.

"I'll have her guess, I'll give her three. A little hope, I'll say, you'll see. If she can guess, she's won the game. How could she win? For Rumpelstiltzkin is my name!"

Queen Ludmila made her escape in quiet haste, back through the tangled paths of fate, to the keep of her castle, where she slept soundly with her child, the raven loitering here and there a top the windowsill. The day following, Ludmila held close to the child through her meals until the moon pushed the sun out of the sky once again, a third since evil's hand had come to claim her. As the castle settled in slumber, clouds covered the land, blocking out the eyes of the heavens. Evil moves amongst the shadows, and, at a flash of lightening, the raven leapt from the windowsill into the starless night sky.

Queen Ludmila, carrying the child, shuffled through the halls towards the storeroom, tense with uncertainty, but certain advantage she owned. Opening now the heavy door, greeted by evil's sour breath, Ludmila paused. Evil's noxious emission bled into the hall. Ludmila, nerved in myelin steel, pushed into the smog of Nuck with the child in her arms.

"Have you now the child in arms, ready to submit? Pass her here, our deal is done, as is right and fit."

"Goblin, no! You mustn't? The child is innocent and true. In her lies hope, the last we have. I'm yours! Take me. You I will obey. Leave the child, your slave I'll be this day."

The elf begins to vibrate, ever faster, with ever more fury, a glowing about him, the room begins to heat. Then his vibration settles, and a wide squinted merry twinkling murderous smile opens lips to sharpened teeth and wormy tongue. A slow staccato cack crackles. Lips press, cheeks puff, switch flick, and the elf booms in maddened joy.

"Guess my name, you tyrant's whore! Guess my name! The child is yours. Guess my name! We'll meet no more!"

And with his proposal, a strung was plucked on the web of fate. Ludmila, the miller's daughter, Queen of the East and her tormentor, a soul twisted by the curse of Nuck, succumbed to the wave and harmonized to the key of destiny. The Queen did not quail, as the goblin had expected. Was that a curl at the corner of her lip? "I think it begins with an R, elf man, I can feel it in my bones!"

The goblin gasped and bared his upper incisors, looking the ass. "Not a Ri-

kalus or a Ramsboord. Or an Regan or Re-
pine. A Rass, a Rammer, Rhone, Remasque,
a Rouge or an Raquorqet. You evil rogue,
I know you and I'll beat you at your game.
For I have hold upon your soul, a power
I will claim, as I isolate the evil - Rumpelstiltzkin is your name!"

See the goblin shake! A tension builds
in every nerve and fibre in his face. He
pushes blood into his skull, and the vibration begins, first in the head, soon the core
and limbs, he's reddening, maddening, soon
to explode. He arches his shoulder blades,
baring his chest, throwing his head back,
roaring to the heavens an primordial syllable
of defeat, plucking a string on the web yet
again. The goblin launches thrice his height
from the floor, plummets impossibly, like
a bolt of darkened lightening, plunging his

left leg to the hip into the stone floor with a mighty boom. Roaring in rage, the elf plants his right leg on the floor between two prepared arms, pushes with an furious evil, tearing the left from his hip with a thunderous roar, waking the gods and anointing the tale of Rumpelstiltzkin to the pantheon legend of lore.

The candle settled to steady flicker, as candles do. Mother turned to her child, smiled, took her hand, and led her on to the dark paths of forever forgotten, forever more.

The End

Goldilocks

Of all the advantages that are bestowed upon a child, none are as insidious as beauty. The ugly child earns his social pleasures through trial and toil. His failures only enhance the sensation of success. The beautiful child is the loved child. First impressions are lasting, and as the world smiles at the child, the child smiles back.

Moral true North is never properly established for the beautiful, for their trespasses are less aggrieving. For ugly, the path of moral integrity is frighteningly narrow, dropping steeply to abyss on either side. Pretty can roller skate drunk and blindfolded in a kindergarten, yet still be considered acceptably moral. Ugly will be okay. It's just a broken ankle. How stupid of him to be in the way.

Pretty has a different name in each story there is to tell, and in this one her name happens to be Tiffany Isabella Tatiana Sinclear. The boys she spurned and the girls, sweating green envy, thought of a clever nickname for her, I wonder can you guess? Her being a mouthful, she was commonly referred to by her long luxurious hair, as Goldilocks. Hi Goldie. Everyone is so happy to meet you, you lucky girl.

Parenting was strange and foreign to the Sinclears. A baby for 5 minutes is an ice cream like treat. A baby for 5 years is intolerable. The child's basic needs were met, she was paraded triumphantly among guests, but when the bright lights dimmed and the spectators withdrew, Tiffany was to be tucked away in a cupboard like a kettle. Goldie grew up feral. Food was on the table at regular hours, but Goldie came and went as she pleased, sometimes pausing her self serving escapades just long enough to wring some silver out of the fleeting spectres that passed as her mother and father.

"But I want it! You will give it me!"

And give it they would, caring more for tonight's fish than their selfish daughter. Everything would turn out just fine for her, for she has been kissed by the angel of fortune. Which is true. With everyone so willing to help, how could she but succeed.

I must apologize. I have been very unkind to our young heroine. I get carried away, for I am prejudiced against her. What has she done to deserve the slander I have heaped upon her? I haven't supported my claims thus far, and I shouldn't paint fair Goldilocks entirely in black. Though selfish by nature, she could work well with others, provided they did what she said. She liked to shine, and worked for praise when it suited her to do so. Impetuous, indeed, impertinent on occasion, but well mannered when being so was important, and often enthusiastic in her doings. There, there, Goldie. You're a sweet girl. What a charming pout!

All this to sow the seeds of doubt in the reader's mind. What is Goldilocks? How are we to stand in judgment of this misguided tale? Is she a poor neglected child, understandably finding her way into trouble? Is she sweet and saintly, as she would have you believe, and in her innocence she has mounted a sacred cow, lucky to escape with her honour and her life? Is she a menace? Should she be shackled and beat?

Goldie was blissfully unaware of the perils that preyed along her very path, and the import they would have as an eternal echo. As far as she was concerned any and all paths were for her choosing, and she may walk where she pleased. Applaud as she goes if you agree, for the sake of proper appearances, appearances befitting a fabled princess.

And go she did one early morn, humming a lullaby, along one of these paths into the fog of a vast forest, said to be peopled by genies and sprites and fairies of all sorts. Handy excuses are in ready supply for the husband that arrives home late and dishevelled. It's the truth, too, if you squint.

What was she to find in the depths of that darkened forest? Love, romance and passion? Sage soulful wisdom? Innocence to experience? An ascension into a pantheon of legends?

Forests begin abruptly, and within a song one can become completely lost. Goldie would sometimes become lost in a grocer's, so we'll forgive her for not recounting exactly where she went. Does that mean that she is useless as an witness to her life? Far from it. Her recollection is in experience, encounters, emotions and impressions, and she was a trouve of useful material.

As the lullaby concluded, the thick quiet of the forest engulfed our heroine. Goldie felt herself naked a moment, and submissively allowed the dictates of destiny to direct her.

A cricket jumped up and danced on her shoe. He bid her a gracious 'miss, how do you do?' With a bow and a scrape, he hopped clear once again, letting Goldie's excursion ensue.

She'd been this way and that, and one stone looked much like another. An adventure turned fretful, Goldie knew not where she was, nor where she might be going. Trying to keep all the trees on a line on her right, losing her line, and then trying all the ones on the left, hopelessly entangled in a web she weaves herself, until finally Miss Goldie happens upon a queer little cottage set apart in the bush.

"What a queer little cottage," exclaims Goldie to herself. "I'll go in, have a look."

Was the door open? It was unlocked, yes, over the threshold, and she's in. In a kitchen. With a table, as one might expect.

But not a table like this. Three frightening bear legs held a carved table top, inset with bear teeth. There was a reddish stain to the wood in many places, making a horrific macabre impression on sensitive Goldie, who suffered a shiver of piano key scales to run up and down her spine, collapsing her in the nearest chair.

The chair was also carved she noticed. Carved with delicate care. Carved with the inspiration of the gods. And on a place mat in front of dear Goldie lay a porcelain portion of apparently pumpkin soup. Could be carrot, thought Goldie. A few handsome sprigs of parsley garnished with appeal. Three settings. Goldie picked up the spoon.

With effort, as the spoon was cast iron. "Cold," thought Goldie and spied a bowl beside, steam rising, the spoon a finely hammered silver. "Ha, Hot!". One more try, and it's just right. She gobbled up the bowl without a thought, a delicious pumpkin, and Goldie throws up a fist of achievement.

Time for a snoop. Goldilocks rummages about, in a delicate, girlish way, not the rampaging male buffoon, but the deft ascertion of all secrets, and the room remained, to all inspection, untouched.

The immediate fear of her situation had well subsided since the soup. The snoop was a thrill, and she threw herself into a chair with a crack. "Aach!" The ache in her back! The chair was as hard as a rock. It was, indeed, a rock, cunningly carved and stained to a wood. "Poof!" she sunk into a cloud, suffocating the struggling girl. "Ah," sighed Goldie on the third chair, "just right." Goldie pumps a fist of success, and the unfortunate chair, as fine as it might be, collapses under the slight celebration of Miss Gold.

After sometime ruminating in her narrow mind, Miss Goldilocks, burn her at the stake, decides she is falling in love with this third bear. Sharing sensibilities much to her liking, she had a burning desire to know more about this pauper prince charming, in the woods, a master artist, undiscovered and pure. She scampered up the steps. Into the bedroom.

Once again there were three. Cautious and knowing, Goldie drags the pads of her fine white fingers over the first, stony dark bed. And again over the pure fur of the second. Goldie lay atop the final bed, rolling with a close eyed smile, under the covers until she was curled right up in her lover's cocoon. And soon was sound aslumber.

The door opens, sometime later, and home come the family. The soup marks a surprise. The chair an outrage, it took weeks to carve. Villain! And the worst was yet to come. But come it does, and now. The Bears find a woman, a child, a doll, sleeping soundly in the third bed.

Papa Bear races, enraged, to the encroacher, latching on to her with his powerful hands. The others are a flutter of limbs in a chaos, as screeching Goldie progresses to beseeching martyr on her way to the door. To the door there's a roar! And another fierce roar, and a savage and scathing abuse as Goldie is tossed on the floor. Papa pushes Goldie out, and shakes fate with the slam and a final roar behind the closing of this tale's door.

The End

Acknowledgments

Who's up next to get some thanks from quarters it's not want? This soap box is the perfect spot from which my thanks to flaunt. There's my family over there, looking sick and gaunt. Methinks my thanks, though it's legit, has the sound of a smirking taunt.

I see you ducking from the words, pretending you can't hear, wary of the backhand praise in retributive fear. Don't worry so, we won't name names, you're safe, you're in the clear. My name attached to yours will not your reputation smear.

But thanks I'll give, cause it's deserved, without you I'd be lost. Your influence has pressed on me, on me you are embossed. And though I've often shuddered from your callous, heartless frost, I'm more than willing, to know you more, to suffer any cost.

Acknowledgment I'll give to you, my blood, my family. Admit, though it's not perfect, that we've nurtured quite a tree. The branches splay out all directions in wondrous variety. This thanks is all for you, without you I'd not be me.

I like me quite a lot, although I know quite well you don't. If you'd prefer I'd quiet down, let's be clear, I won't.

Author

    The inception of a mythos we have buried back in time. Story follows story, and corrupts it line by line. I'm adding fuel upon a pyre to keep a memory lit. Change it does what's come before, don't tell me that's a crime. Jack had all but wedding rings. Bo found a man that fit. Red defeated semi-evil and kept a little bit. Goldi trapsed on property and got away scot free. Rumpelstiltzkin's faithful to his type, so don't blame me. Perhaps the miller's daughter isn't what you thought she'd be. But it's just another branch you'll find that's growing on the tree.

    Fairie Tales are living, they will last beyond us all. Aesop taught us much with just a tortoise that could crawl. You can bet I've got a Cinderella coming to the ball. But don't expect the whole damn lot, just a dozen heard the call. More there are, than I can count, red bricks upon this wall.

These bricks have built a cathedral. I could move on and leave it at that, and you'd take it and not think much of it. I'm not going to do that. I'm not going to move on. You're going to stop and have a good long look here at this structure.

The greatest artist of his time, whichever one you choose, created his thing, or handful of things. A cathedral is a considerable investment of capital collected and dispersed to congregate the greatest tradesmen of their day and set them to work on a single project for a significant portion of their very lives. The best in their respective fields, collaborating to create one final product over a generation. Damn! Those buildings are cool.

I want to be a builder. I want to set some of those bricks. Just some unobstructive ones, not much seen. I won't collapse the whole structure, or even damage any part of it. Just a few little bricks on top. Like Halloween decoration. You can take them off later, no problem. Let me die first.

Hell's Press

In prison does a man reside, a punishment for birth. Suffer, will he, while he's here, to fate's eternal mirth. He may well wonder, time to time, what life is really worth. Why must he wander, lonely, to his grave beneath the earth. But never while he's curled up, cozy, on a rug beside the hearth.

Printed in the USA
CPSIA information can be obtained
at www.ICGtesting.com
JSHW081729081123
51651JS00004B/147